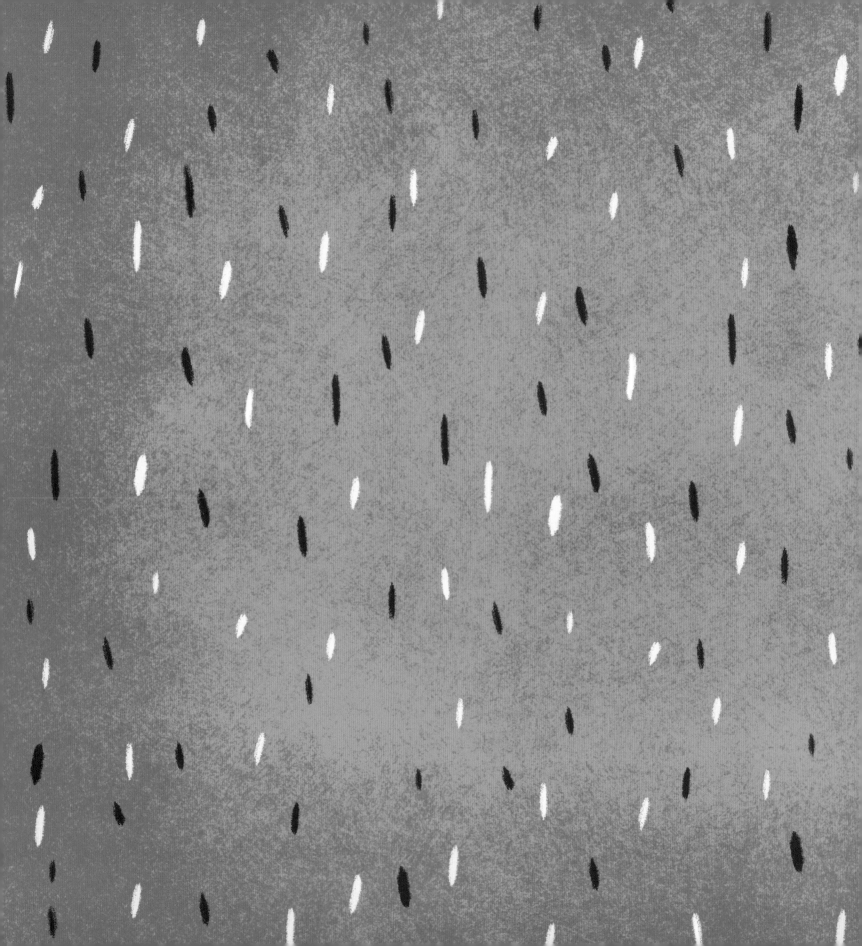

For Maya, Mahi and Mika

First published in 2020 by Child's Play (International) Ltd
Ashworth Road, Bridgemead, Swindon SN5 7YD, UK

First published in 2020 in USA by Child's Play Inc
250 Minot Avenue, Auburn, Maine 04210

Distributed in Australia by Child's Play Australia Pty Ltd
Unit 10/20 Narabang Way, Belrose, Sydney, NSW 2085

ISBN 978-1-78628-087-9
CLP190819CPL10190879

Printed in Shenzhen, China

1 3 5 7 9 10 8 6 4 2

A catalogue record of this book
is available from the British Library

www.childs-play.com

Max + Xam

Ariane Hofmann-Maniyar

Max and Xam were next-door neighbors.

They both loved
spending time together.

But one day, things went a bit wild.

You started it!

No I didn't!

Oh yes you did!

You said you had lots more friends than me!

So what? That's TRUE!

After this, things changed.

No more afternoon teas.

No more sweet dreams!

But Max had a plan!

Max gathered this...

and Max gathered that.

Then Max got to work.

Max made lots of new friends!

Xam
also had
a plan.

Xam made lots of new friends too.

Even more than Max.

That afternoon, Max made
tea for all the new friends.

But no one ate.

That evening, Xam wished all the new friends sweet dreams.

But no one replied.

Max missed Xam.

Xam missed Max.

Finally, Max was tired of being upset with Xam
and set off with plates full of their favorite treats.

Xam felt the same, so chose the most beautiful flowers from the garden.

My favorite flowers!

My favorite cake!

My favorite friend!